5 Islamic Stories for Children

By Muhammad Iqbal

Contents

Story 1 – Charity & Thankfullness to Allaah

Imran was excited. His Father was taking him to the new shopping centre that had opened up in his city for the first time! It was the special opening weekend and he was sure there would be lots of cool things to see, his Father might even buy him a new scooter!

It was a hot, sunny day. Imran's Father eventually parked up in the brand new parking area. And they left the car to enter the new shopping centre.

On the way Imran noticed what looked like a man lying down near one of the pillars in the distance.

"Amazing!" he thought to himself, "People are even more excited than me, they have been waiting the whole night for the shopping centre to open!"

Imran ran ahead into the centre. Once inside, it was more than he had imagined! The shiny white floors and glass roof which let the sun in made him feel like he was in a palace. There were decorations everywhere, "What a great place" he thought to himself. There were clothes shops, food shops, pet shops and most importantly to Imran, toy stores!

The day continued on. To Imran's great surprise, his Father was so impressed by his Son's patience and good behaviour throughout the day that he bought him the scooter he wanted so much! *"Alhamdulilaah"* Imran said to himself, thankful for getting what we wanted.

After praying *Asr Salaah*, Imran's Father decided it would be best to make their way home. Excited to ride his new scooter in the garden, Imran happily agreed. Shortly after exiting the shopping centre, something caught Imran's eye. He turned and noticed the same man lying next to the pillar in the distance.

This time, Imran stopped in his tracks. He knew something wasn't right.

"Dad", he said curiously. "Why is that man still there? Does he not know that the centre is open?"

"What do you mean Imran?" replied his Father.

Imran explained. "When we first came here this morning, I saw this man in the same place. Now we are leaving and he is still there, he hasn't moved!"

"My Son", Imran's Father said softly, "This man is someone who is homeless. He doesn't have a house because he is poor".

Imran felt a gap in his heart. How could someone be so poor that they didn't have a home? Imran had a home, he had a bed and he even had a new scooter he wanted so much. But this man had nothing. He didn't even have the benefit of a warm, soft bed.

The journey home was difficult for Imran. He never would have imagined that people lived like this. Slowly, he started to realise how many things he had in his life that he never thanked Allaah for.

He had somewhere to live where he was safe. He had a Mother and Father to take care of him. He had eyes with which he could see the world around him. He had ears that worked and allowed him to hear his Mother call his name.

The longer the thought, the more he realised that the list of blessings he had were endless.

"*Alhamdulilaah*" he said to himself. "Allaah has given me so many blessings that I should be grateful for."

He had food which was prepared by his parents for him day and night. His clothes were washed and replaced when they were worn, he had the most comfortable bed to sleep in as he wished. What more could he ask for?

The more Imran pondered his blessings, the more sadness he felt for the homeless man he saw at the centre that day. For everything he had, the poor man did not have.

Later that evening, Imran had an idea.

"Mum, Dad – can I ask for a favour?"

"What is it Imran?" His father replied.

The night was cold and quiet, Imran's father was driving through the roads with Imran and his mother in the back seat. At last they had arrived. Imran and his Parents approached the homeless man they saw earlier outside the shopping centre.

"*As salaamu alaykum*" Imran's father said to the man.

"*Wa 'alaykum salaam*" replied the man, curious as to why he had been approached by a man, his wife and their son so late at night.

"This is for you, my son saw you earlier and wanted us to give this to you" said Imran's father gently as he handed over a bag full of food, clothes and blankets.

"Thank you. May Allaah bless you with much good!" said the man, clearly overjoyed.

As Imran and his parents were leaving, Imran looked back and saw the man pulling his new blanket over him and eating from his newly arrived food.

"You did a very good thing today Imran" said his father. "I think I have even learnt a very valuable lesson from you".

Full of happiness, Imran hugged both his parents and reminded himself always to be grateful for his blessings and to help those in need.

Lessons Learnt:

- Always be kind and courteous to the poor

- It is a sign of good character to remember the poor and to give charity frequently

- Remember to thank Allaah for all the blessings you have, there are always others who may not have the things you take for granted

Qur'aan:

Allaah Says in the Qur'aan:

"...And if you should count the favor of Allaah, you could not enumerate them..." [1]

Message from the Author:

My dear brothers and sisters in Islam, always be grateful for what Allaah has given you. Even if you think you do not have much, thank Allaah for your health, your hearing, your sight and so on.

If Allaah has blessed you with wealth, then do not forget the poor and those less well off. It is our duty as Muslims to always be helping each other and the less fortunate.

Story 2 – Parents

It was a hot, sunny day. Yahya didn't like the heat, he especially didn't enjoy waiting while his Mother shopped in the stalls behind him. The market was far too busy for him. People were walking up and down the street to buy what they needed. Yahya wasn't bothered by all of that – he just wanted to go home!

He would much rather be playing with his Brother or even running around in his garden. Even his homework seemed interesting compared to sitting outside the shop.

While he was busy daydreaming of everything he would rather be doing, he noticed a cat on the other side of the street purring at passers-by. This wasn't unusual, but it got his attention. Not long after, he saw someone give the cat some meat. What was unusual however, was that the cat didn't eat it, it held it in its mouth and walked off.

"That was weird" he thought. But nothing too strange, he had never felt this bored before and couldn't wait to get home!

A few minutes passed. To Yahya it felt like a few hours, when suddenly he heard more purring. This time closer by. He turned to see where it was coming from, and it was the same cat purring at more passers-by, this time on his side of the street.

"What a greedy cat" he said to himself. "She had food, now she wants more!"

Again, the cat was given some meat and again she picked it up by her teeth and scampered off.

Yahya felt something was not quite right about this. Why was the cat not eating the food, but taking it and then coming back for more?

Suddenly, and just as Yahya expected, the cat again returned to the street for the third time purring for more food. This time, Yahya's curiosity got the better of him. He waited for the cat to be given some more meat, which it did almost immediately. As it walked off, Yahya got up and followed.

It twisted and turned through the different stalls, Yahya almost felt dizzy following it! He lost sight of it for a second but then saw it again, it was hard to keep up!

Finally he saw the cat turn the corner, after following he immediately stopped. Before him the cat he had been following was giving the meat it had to its baby kittens! Yahya watched silently as the cat split the meat into smaller pieces and fed it to the kittens. One by one they all ate it up. "This cat must be their Mother!" he thought to himself excitedly.

"That's weird", then thought Yahya to himself, "What about the Mother Cat? Isn't she hungry too?"

He had noticed that in all the eating, the Mother Cat had not touched the meat after she split it for her kittens. Normally Yahya would have thought that maybe the Mother Cat was not hungry, but when he looked at her more closely, he could see that her ribs were almost showing through her skin!

"*SubhaanAllaah*", he wondered. "This Mother Cat is feeding her children even though she is hungry herself. She splits the food and watches her children eat it without her even though she is hungry!"

It was then that Yahya thought of his own Mother. How many times had she made food for him and he didn't eat it? How often did she carry an umbrella to shield him from the rain while getting wet herself? How many times had he run to his Mothers room in the night hungry and she had went to their kitchen to make him food?

Tears slowly started to build up in the corners of his eyes. There was so much his Mother had done for him and he never once appreciated it. In fact he didn't even realise it. He slowly and quietly raised his hands to make *du'aa*, making sure not to startle the Mother Cat and her kittens.

"O' Allaah, bless my Parents for taking care of me when I was small and helpless"

No sooner had he lowered his hands when he felt a soft touch on his shoulder.

"Yahya! There you are!" His Mother said. "I was worried about where you had run off to!"

At this the Mother Cat and her kittens ran off, leaving Yahya and his Mother.

"I'm sorry Mum, I was following a cat and then…"

"Don't worry my love" his Mother gently replied. "You didn't go too far, I'm glad I saw you when I did. I was beginning to panic!"

Yahya and his Mother both turned to make their journey home.

"How about we get some of your favourite Ice Cream? I have some money left over from today's shopping" Yahya's Mother suggested.

Yahya remembered how eager the Mother Cat was to feed her children and immediately felt humbled. Being a Parent must be hard work, and now Yahya loved his Mother even more.

"Thank you for taking care of me Mum, I love you" he said gently to his Mother.

"That's very sweet of you Yahya" she said.

"I love you too".

Lesson Learnt:

- Our Parents take care of us like no one else in the world, they put their needs before ours

- We must respect, love and cherish our Parents entirely

- We must love and respect our Parents

Qur'aan:

Allaah Says in the Qur'aan:

"And we have enjoined on man to be good and dutiful to his parents" [2]

Message from the Author:

My dear brothers and sisters, our Parents took care of us when we were small and helpless. We could not even lift our heads or sit up but our Parents did it for us.

Allaah has placed great importance on treating our Parents kindly and with respect, dignity and honour. As we grow older and mature, our Parents grow older and weaker. It is one of our most important duties to make sure we take care of our Parents as much as possible.

Story 3 – Good Manners and Being Kind

Maryam was excited. She did her homework on time but didn't always enjoy it. But today was different. After a long day at school, her teacher had given her class homework that she couldn't wait to do.

Her task was to colour in the most beautiful picture of a masjid. She imagined filling in the brilliant golden dome, and surrounding the masjid with green grass. She skipped home excitedly while holding onto her Father's hand.

Upon reaching home she hurried in, prayed Salaat al 'Asr and got her crayons ready. How she loved her brand new crayons! As she was sitting down, the door creaked open and her baby brother Umar came in.

Maryam loved Umar, but she felt he could be a bit annoying sometimes. Umar was only 3 years old, he too loved crayons and when he saw Maryam get them out ready to colour in he rushed in to join her.

Right away he wanted to join in. Maryam immediately called out:

"Mummy!"

"Yes Maryam?" replied her Mother.

"Umar is trying to join in and is not letting me use the crayons!"

"You must learn to share Maryam, why don't you give him a blank sheet of paper and let him do his own colouring in with you?"

Maryam listened, her Mother was right.

Umar would be able to draw on his own sheet, and Maryam could finish her homework in peace.

As the minutes went by and the page filled up with beautiful colours, Maryam had only the golden dome and the green grass to finish. No sooner had she picked up the yellow crayon had Umar taken it from her!

"Fine", she thought. "Ill start with the grass instead".

She picked up the green crayon and started drawing. All of a sudden, Umar took that out of her hand too!

It was clear to Maryam that Umar was jealous and wanted whatever she was using.

"Why cant you just draw on your own paper?!" She snapped loudly.

Umar's happy expression faded and his mouth curled as he began to cry.

Maryam's Mother came into the room.

"Mum!" explained Maryam, "Umar keeps taking my crayons and snatching them off me when I try to colour in. I can't do my homework!"

After comforting Umar and wiping away his tears, Maryam's Mother spoke to her.

"Umar is your younger Brother and gets excited to see you and play with you. He waits all day at home while you are at school asking when you will come back. Try and be nice with him, he doesn't fully understand yet"

These words felt very heavy to Maryam, but she understood. Umar was half her age and always joined in with whatever Maryam was doing. Not to annoy her, as Maryam previously thought, but to have fun with her.

She was his fun, big sister and if he couldn't rely on her to have fun, who else was there?

"Come with me" Maryam's Mother said to Umar as she led him out of the room to give Maryam some space. "You can help me tidy your room"

"..Wait!" Maryam called.

"What is it Maryam?" her Mother replied.

"..I'm sorry for being annoyed with you Umar" She said softly. "Do you want to help me finish off the rest of my homework?"

Umar's face lit up in joy. He rushed over and picked up a crayon.

"Lets work together" Maryam said. "You colour in the grass green, but try and stay within the lines. Can you do that?" She asked.

"Yes!" replied Umar happily.

Maryam's Mother smiled and walked out of the room.

Maryam noticed Umar colour outside of the lines every so often, but Maryam reminded herself to remain patient. Umar was half her age and was doing her best to help her. She gave him a big smile which he returned with an even bigger one.

Later that evening after Salaat al Maghrib, the colouring in was complete. The golden dome and fresh green grass were all coloured in. Maryam noticed that Umar had slightly gone out of the lines in some places, but this didn't matter to her now.

The drawing didn't look exactly as she had planned but Maryam wasn't sad. In fact she was happy. She had a fun afternoon with her baby Brother and she was patient with him. In that one afternoon she realised the more important lesson of the day.

Being patient and having good manners with others.

"You are the best Sister ever." Umar said tiredly as he fell asleep.

"And you are the best Brother ever" She replied happily.

-

<u>Lessons Learnt:</u>

- Be patient when you deal with others, especially when it may be your family members

- Teamwork is often better and a lot more fun than doing a job alone

- Always think the best of others, try and see things from their point of view

<u>Hadeeth:</u>

The Prophet (peace and blessings of Allaah be upon him) said:

"Indeed the most beloved of you to me is the best of you in manners." [3]

<u>Message from the Author:</u>

My dear brothers and sisters in Islam. Remember to be patient and have good manners with people, especially your family.

Always try and understand that things might not always be what they seem. You may deal with someone who is upset at something else and they might be upset towards you. Being patient and understanding with them will only draw them closer to you.

And Allaah loves the patient ones.

Story 4 – Telling the Truth & Being Fair

Abdullah and Jameelah couldn't wait to get home. They had gone out with their Mother to the supermarket and they had been rewarded for their good behaviour with a toy they were very excited about. A big, red, shiny ball!

Finally they arrived at home, Jameelah's Mother told her and Abdullah to get dressed into their home clothes and wait for her to finish putting the shopping away, they were not allowed to play with the ball yet.

Abdullah and Jameelah waited, the ball was next to them and they didn't touch it. But after 10 minutes, Abdullah lost his patience and took the ball. He began bouncing it on the floor, it made a sound but he was sure that his Mother couldn't hear it from the other room.

"Throw it to me Abdullah!" Jameelah shouted. Jameelah and her older brother Abdullah were excited to play with their new ball! Abdullah and Jameelah ran around the house, the ball bouncing off their living room table into Jameelah's hands. They couldn't remember the last time they had this much fun!

After moving into the Hallway, Adam asked Jameelah to throw it back to him. Jameelah, having such a good time did. This time however, the ball had missed Abdullah and headed for their Mother's beloved flowerpot on a shelf!

SMASH

All of a sudden, they could both hear footsteps rushing towards them. It was their Mother! Surely they would be in big trouble now!

Abdullah and his sister ran into the Living Room, what would they do? What would they say?

But there was no time to think. Their Mother came into the Hallway and saw her favourite flowerpot broken on the ground, smashed into pieces.

"What happened?!?" She said both angry and upset. "Who did this?"

"N..Nothing Mum, it wasn't me!" replied Abdullah. He was clearly very afraid for what he and Jameelah had done, if only they had listened and not touched the ball without permission!

Jameelah was too worried to say anything, until her brother also said "It was Jameelah! She threw the ball and it broke the flowerpot!"

At this, Jameelah's Mother looked at her, her face very upset. Jameelah tried to answer her brother back saying that it wasn't her fault, after all, wasn't Abdullah the one to take the ball when he shouldn't have? It was so unfair!

"Jameelah, I am very disappointed with you." Her Mother continued, "You are not allowed to play with your toys until tomorrow, this is your punishment.

Jameelah started to cry. Her Mother then swept up the shattered pieces of her favourite flowerpot from the floor and cleared the floor. It all felt so unfair, her brother had taken the ball, started the game and blamed it all on her. To top it all off, she couldn't play with her toys for the rest of the evening!

Abdullah was looking at his little sister. Did Jameelah really deserve all of the blame? Was this the full truth? Abdullah's Father had always told him to tell the truth.

All of a sudden, he stood up and left the room. He went to his Mother, held her hand and brought her into the Living Room where Jameelah was crying silently.

"Mum, I am sorry your flowerpot was broken. I want to tell you the truth about what happened, it wasn't just Jameelah's fault.

I took the ball from the bag when you told us not to, I was being impatient and was too excited. I started throwing the ball back and forth with Jameelah. I asked her to throw it back to me but she missed and it hit the flowerpot. That was how it ended up being broken.

It's my fault too and I am sorry"

Feeling ashamed, Abdullah hung his head. Expecting a big telling off from his Mother, he was surprised when he felt a big hug that squashed both him and Jameelah together.

"Thank you for telling the truth Abdullah", his Mother said.

"I did love that flowerpot, but I love good manners and telling the truth more." Their Mother explained.

"Besides" she smiled "I can always buy another flowerpot."

Both Adam and Jameelah smiled, Jameelah's Mother wiped away her tears and gave a smile that lit up the whole room.

"One more thing" Abdullah said. "Jameelah, I'm sorry for blaming you so quickly. I was the one to take the ball and I shouldn't have done that"

"I have an idea" their Mother said. "You two take the ball and go and play in the garden until Maghrib Salaah, I will bake you both a nice chocolate pudding for dessert!"

Adam and Jameelah were overjoyed. Telling the truth seemed like the best choice after all!

-

<u>Lessons Learnt:</u>

- Always tell the truth, even if it means you get into trouble

- Even when you can blame someone else for something you did wrong, understand that it is the wrong thing to do. Allaah is Watching over you.

- Be fair with others and take responsibility for your actions

<u>Hadeeth:</u>

The Messenger of Allaah (blessings and peace of Allaah be upon him) said:

"Truth leads to piety and piety leads to Jannah. A man persists in speaking the truth till he is enrolled with Allaah as a truthful.

Falsehood leads to vice and vice leads to the Fire (Hell), and a person persists on telling lies until he is enrolled as a liar". [4]

<u>Message from the Author:</u>

My young brothers and sisters in Islam. Always tell the truth and don't be afraid.

There may be times in your life where you feel that telling a lie will make things easier for you, but it is the wrong thing to do. Once you tell a lie, it becomes easier to tell another lie, and so on and so on.

The same happens with telling the truth. Always do it and you will see how it becomes easier and easier.

Remember that Allaah loves those who are truthful.

Story 5 – Kindness to Neighbours

Eesa sat still on the sofa watching the clock ticking by.

He could hear the clinking of pans from the kitchen and the smell of his Mum's cooking made his tummy rumble. But he wasn't waiting for dinnertime, he counted the seconds as the clock ticked to 5 o'clock and just on time, he jumped up and ran to the hallway where his trainers were.

Careful to tie his laces, Eesa stood up and peered below at his shoes. They stared back - tired, dirty and old, they often hurt if he lent to one side a bit too much. Eesa remembered how bright and perfect they were when his Father surprised him with them a few years ago for Eid; a smile stretched his face as his trainers wearily ran along with him to the kitchen to say goodbye to his Mother.

Waiting outside was Eesa's best friend Adam. Adam lived just next door to Eesa and every Saturday, Eesa would wait anxiously until 5 o'clock when he and Adam would play a game of football. Eesa loved to play with Adam and looked forward to the time they could spend together. Adam was just a little older than Eesa and slightly taller. He had more brothers and sisters than Eesa and they seemed not to like their trainers very much.

Eesa thought this because every week Adam would always wear a new pair of trainers he'd never seen before! He told Eesa that his brothers gave them to him and Eesa wondered for a moment what it would be like to have an older brother like that.

Today was no different. Adam stood with a pair of red trainers, one foot balanced over a matching shiny red ball. Eesa ran to Adam and said gave *salaam*.

They kicked the ball to one another, Eesa tried different angles of his foot to get the ball to spin just like Adam knew. "Use the inside of your foot like this!" Adam advised, offering Eesa a chance. Eesa kept trying for what only seemed like a short time before his Mother came to call him for dinner.

"But Mum!" Eesa protested, trying to think of a good reason to be late for dinner "No" his Mum said, as though she knew what Eesa was thinking.

Eesa turned to Adam to say goodbye when he saw Adam's nose lifted in the air towards Eesa's house. Adam took a long sniff as he closed his eyes, his mouth smiling ever so slightly. "Is that chocolate cake?" asked Adam, opening his eyes brightly towards Eesa's Mum.

Eesa looked at Adam and then his Mum who stood holding a foil wrapped plate infront of her. "Here, take this to your Mother and give her my *salaam*" his Mother said warmly, crouching down to make sure Adam held the plate well enough. Adam's smile was now a huge one, showcasing all of his teeth and the few that were missing.

Eesa looked at his Mother, his mouth watering slightly as Adam held the cake. "Can you please help Adam take this to his Mother?" she asked, turning to look at him. Eesa nodded slowly, hoping there would be some cake left for him too.

He and Adam walked together and knocked on Adam's door. Adam's Mum opened the door and glanced at the plate then at Eesa.

"Is this from your Mum, Eesa darling?" she asked, her voice rose in surprise as she took the plate from her son! "Oh my boy! Isn't your Mother so lovely!" Eesa nodded and agreed, he thought his Mum was lovely too! She laughed from what seemed like her heart and suddenly stopped.

Her eyes widened and she turned to call Adam's brother from inside "Can you please get me the box next to the sofa?" she asked as Eesa heard small footsteps scuttling away. When she was given the box, she handed it over to him. "Here Eesa darling! These are for you!" she said, smiling brightly.

He had hardly opened the box fully before he realised what was inside. A brand new pair of trainers just like the ones he had always wanted!

Eesa was overjoyed, he couldn't believe what he was holding! He ran back home to tell his Mother the good news. As he proudly displayed the gift he received from Adam's family to his Mother, he noticed a smile grow proudly across her face.

"May Allaah bless our neighbours!" she said happily.

That evening Eesa's house was one of joy and happiness. His Mother had invited Adam's Mother over for dinner after *Salaat al Ishaa* and they exchanged stories and laughed throughout the night.

Lessons Learnt:

- Always be kind and polite to your neighbours
- Your neighbours have many rights over you, don't forget about them
- Giving gifts is a good way to increase love between people

Hadeeth:

The Prophet (peace and blessings of Allaah be upon him) said:

"The best of companions with Allaah is the one who is best to his companions, and the best of neighbours to Allaah is the one who is the best of them to his neighbour". [5]

Message from the Author:

My dear young Muslim, our Prophet (peace and blessings of Allaah be upon him) taught us about treating our neighbours in a good manner, even if they are not Muslim.

We live in times where people may go weeks or years without even knowing who their neighbours are, but we should establish good relations with them even so.

Always remember that you are showing your good manners and representing Islam when you see them and meet them.

Let them find in you a shining example.

References

[1]Surah Ibraaheem, Verse 34

[2] (29:8)

[3] Silsilah al-Ahadeeth as-Saheehah' – Shaykh Nasur uddeen al-Albaani (Translated by Abbas Abu Yahya)

[4] Imam Al-Nawawi's Riyad-us-Saliheen, Chapter 4: Truthfulness

[5] Imam Al Nawawi's Riyad-us-Saliheen, Chapter 39: Rights of Neighbors

All hadeeth taken from abdurrahman.org

Glossary

'Asr:

The mid-late afternoon prayer that Muslims are required to pray each day.

-

Alhamdulilaah:

An Arabic phrase meaning 'Praise be to Allaah'. Said in times of happiness, sorrow, grief and joy as a way of remaining happy and grateful to Allaah.

-

As salaamu 'alaykum:

The standard Muslim greeting meaning 'May peace be upon you'.

Du'aa:

Invocation to Allaah/Prayer to God.

Hadeeth:

Narrations from the Prophet (peace and blessings of Allaah be upon him).

-

Maghrib:

The sunset prayer that Muslims are required to pray each day.

-

Salaah/Salaat:

Prayer. This refers to the 5 day prayers that all Muslims must complete daily.

-

Salaam:

Meaning 'peace'. Shorthand for the Islamic greeting 'As salaamu 'alaykum' (May peace be upon you)

SubhaanAllaah:

An Arabic phrase meaning 'Glory be to Allaah'. Said in times of happiness, astonishment, sorrow, grief or joy as a way of reminding oneself of Allaah's magnificence.

-

Surah:

A chapter from the Qur'aan.

Qur'aan:

The Holy scripture of the Muslims. Muslims believe that the Qur'aan was revealed by Allaah to His Prophet (peace and blessings be upon him).

-

Wa 'alaykum salaam:

Meaning 'And upon you be peace'. This is the standard response to the Islamic greeting 'As salaamu 'alaykum'.

Printed in Great Britain
by Amazon